One More Wednesday

by Malika Doray • translated by Suzanne Freeman

GREENWILLOW BOOKS
An Imprint of HarperCollinsPublishers

On Wednesdays

when I was little,

Granny and I baked cakes and cookies.

Then we ate them up.

Sometimes Granny could get grumpy...

but most of the time we had fun.

When I was busy coloring,

I would hear her sing.

Oh . . . and she had a dog named Bobo.

We walked him in the park.

At the end of the day,

waiting for Papa,

I would fall asleep

in Granny's lap.

And as Papa carried me home,

Granny would call out to me,

"See you next Wednesday!"

But then one Wednesday came,

and I couldn't go see Granny.

She was in the hospital.

Later on, the telephone rang,

and Mama cried.

Papa held me and told me:

Granny had died.

We went to her funeral,

but I didn't understand. . . .

Did this mean that

my granny was gone forever?

I asked Mama.

"That's not easy to answer,"

Mama said.

"Some people say

that when you die,

your spirit goes up to heaven.

"Other people say

that when you die,

your spirit comes back

as a new baby, or maybe

as a bird or a bee or even a tree.

"Nobody knows for sure,"
Mama said, "but I'll tell you
what I do know.

"Before you were even born,

in some way you were already here

because we wanted you so much.

"And it's the same with Granny now.

In some way she'll always be here

because you love her so much."

Later we found

a picture of Granny.

Papa gave it a beautiful frame,

and we put it in my room.

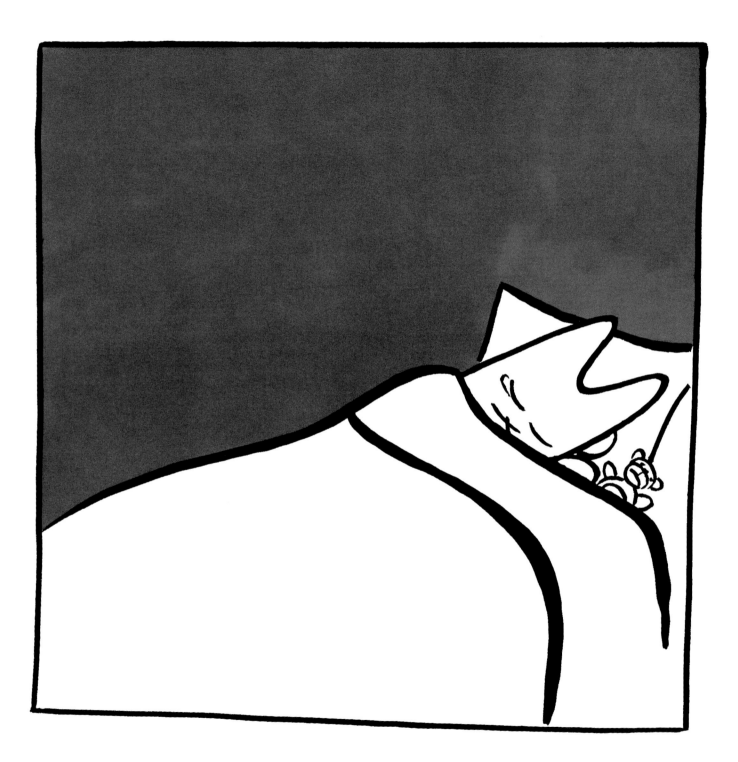

At first, thinking of Granny

made me cry.

But now it's just nice.

Because when I remember her,

I think of her singing.

I think of her warm lap.

And it almost could be

one more Wednesday

with my Granny.

To Aurélia,

For Julie, Coline, Lola, Doris, and Vodia,

With a thousand thanks to Elisabeth,

And love to my Nasturtium and to the field mouse.

With my gratefulness to the 3 Bears for their help,
and to Romain Goupil, for his movie A mort la mort!

One More Wednesday
Copyright © 2001 by Malika Doray
Translation copyright © 2001 by Suzanne Freeman
All rights reserved.
Printed in Singapore by Tien Wah Press.
www.harperchildrens.com

A black brush line and markers
were used to create the full-color art.
The text type is Futura.

Library of Congress Cataloging-in-Publication Data

Doray, Malika.
One more Wednesday / by Malika Doray ; translated from the French by Suzanne Freeman.
p.   cm.
"Greenwillow Books."
Summary: When a little animal's grandmother dies, he remembers
good times with her and asks his mother about death.
ISBN 0-06-029589-9 (trade). ISBN 0-06-029590-2 (lib. bdg.)
[1. Death—Fiction. 2. Grandmothers—Fiction. 3. Animals—Fiction.]
I. Freeman, Suzanne (Suzanne T.).   II. Title.
PZ7.D72738 On 2001   [E]—dc21   00-044288

First Edition 10 9 8 7 6 5 4 3 2 1